D1438886

Stronger
THAN SHE THINKS

Dedicated to my parents, who were always there to help me get back up. —N.K.

Text copyright © 2023 by Nancy Kerrigan and Ryan G. Van Cleave
Illustrations copyright © 2023 by Arief Putra

Published by Bushel & Peck Books, a family-run publishing house in Fresno, California, that believes in uplifting children with the highest standards of art, music, literature, and ideas. Find beautiful books for gifted young minds at www.bushelandpeckbooks.com.

Type set in LTC Kennerley and Rumba

Bushel & Peck Books is dedicated to fighting illiteracy all over the world. For every book we sell, we donate one to a child in need— book for book. To nominate a school or organization to receive free books, please visit www.bushelandpeckbooks.com.

LCCN: 2023944440
ISBN: 978-1-63819-207-7

First Edition

Printed in Canada

1 3 5 7 9 10 8 6 4 2

Stronger
THAN SHE THINKS

NANCY KERRIGAN

WITH RYAN G. VAN CLEAVE · ILLUSTRATED BY ARIEF PUTRA

BUSHEL
& PECK
BOOKS

Nancy was a **racer!**

She **tore** through the neighborhood on a hand-me-down bike.

She **zipped** over the waves of Lake Sunapee.

She **charged** across concrete with a hockey stick.

And at night, she **darted** through her backyard, catching fireflies in her hands. No matter what Nancy did, she

zoomed!

That's why Nancy loved ice skating.
Blasting across the slick rink was

exhilarating!

But figure skating required more than just speed. Dancing on the ice wasn't the same as racing. So, Nancy took lessons.

Nancy's dad worked three jobs, and her mom didn't work outside the home because she was blind. Money was tight, but Nancy's parents found a way.

Come sun, rain, or snow, Nancy's mom and dad took her to the local ice rink for lessons— the same where her dad drove a Zamboni, shaving and smoothing the ice to glistening perfection.

At first, lessons were with a gaggle of kids.

Then with Nancy and a few others.

Then just her.

Nancy skated backward like a **rocket**.

She **streaked** into crossovers and lunges.

She **whizzed** through scratch, sit, and camel spins.

And she jumped.
Wow, was Nancy a

jumper!

Toe loop.

Salchow.

LUTZ.

But try as she might, Nancy couldn't seem to land an axel—the most difficult jump of all. The jump that separated future stars from everyday skaters.

More than anything, Nancy wanted to compete.
She wanted to show a crowd all she could do.
Nancy was sure she was ready, but Coach disagreed.

"You've got to learn
the axel," Coach said.

Nancy was an athlete! Physical activities had never been a challenge . . . until now. Worse, Nancy's feet *hurt*. A growth spurt had left her skates two sizes too small, and the shoe stretcher just wouldn't

s t r e t c h

them any wider.

New skates weren't an option. Figure skating was already so expensive.

Nancy limped home. Her skates weren't going to get any less pinchy. She could either scrunch up her toes and skate through the pain, or she could quit.

"If that's what it takes to keep skating," Nancy told herself, "then that's what I'll do."

So, feet squished into her too-small skates, Nancy returned to the rink.

She grew **cold**.

She felt **achy**.

She turned **black and blue**.

Nancy thought about all the other jumps she *could* do. She thought about her mom clapping for her in the stands. She thought about how it'd feel to stun a crowd with her ability.

Nancy got to her feet.

"I have to go faster," she decided. Speed meant height, and more height meant more time to rotate.

Nancy accelerated until she moved like lightning.

Then she **launched** herself with all her strength . . .

. . . and landed a wobbly axel.

Nancy's next attempt had a solid landing.

The axel after that was solid *and* smooth.

Eventually, landing axel jumps was no harder than lacing up those achy-tight skates.

"*Now* you're ready," Coach told her.

Nancy borrowed a beaded skating dress. She chose a song from the musical *A Chorus Line*. And she worked with Coach to choreograph a routine that showcased speed, power, and acceleration.

And an axel.

Nancy rehearsed until her thighs burned.
She practiced until her knees ached and her
feet throbbed. Then she rehearsed even more.

On the Big Day, Nancy's stomach butterflied.
Was she *really* ready?

Nancy eased into her starting pose.
The music crackled to life . . .

...and Nancy **took off!**

On her old, squeezy skates, she breezed around the rink.

Forward.

Backward.

She transitioned smoothly through crossovers, lunges, and spins.

The music swelled toward her big finish.
Nancy picked up speed. Faster, FASTER!

Nancy took a deep breath,

lifted up her knee,

pushed off the ice,

sprang into the air,

whirled like a top,

and . . .

. . . landed a perfect, graceful axel.

The audience cheered!

Even though it was only parents, family members, and other skaters, to Nancy, it felt as if the whole world was watching. Cameras flashed like fireflies as she took a bow. She rushed over to hug her parents.

"If I'm strong enough to do this," Nancy realized, "I can do . . .

Hello!

I hope you enjoyed reading *Stronger Than She Thinks* as much as I enjoyed making this book. From the earliest moments in my skating career, I faced obstacle after obstacle. But I kept trying. Every time I fell, I got back up. Every time I failed, I tried again. Every time someone told me no, I kept working until I earned a yes.

It helped enormously to have the support of my friends, family, and coaches along the way. But in the end, I was the one who had to dig deep and keep on going. Eventually, I learned that I had more strength within me than I ever realized. And here's great news—you're stronger than you think, too.

Believe in yourself!

Nancy Kerrigan